# Peter Brown

LITTLE, BROWN AND COMPANY

New York · Boston

# For Grumps

Little, Brown and Company

Hachette Book Group USA
1271 Avenue of the Americas, New York, NY 10020
Visit our Web site at www.lb-kids.com

First Edition: September 2006

Library of Congress Cataloging-in-Publication Data

Brown, Peter.
  Chowder / by Peter Brown.— 1st ed.
      p. cm.
  Summary: Chowder the bulldog has never fit in with the other neighborhood canines, but he sees a chance to make friends with the animals at the local petting zoo.
  ISBN-13: 978-0-316-01180-8 (hardcover)
  ISBN-10: 0-316-01180-0 (hardcover)
 [1. Bulldog—Fiction. 2. Dogs—Fiction. 3. Petting zoos—Fiction. 4. Animals—Fiction.]
I. Title.
PZ7.B81668Cho 2006
[Fic]—dc22
                                                    2005035616


10  9  8  7  6  5  4  3  2

SC

Manufactured in China

Book design by Tracy Shaw

The illustrations for this book were done in acrylic and pencil on board.
The text was set in Nimrod, and the display type is Kon Tiki Trader.

Chowder had always been **different**.

His owners liked to think of him as quirky,
but most people thought he was just plain weird.

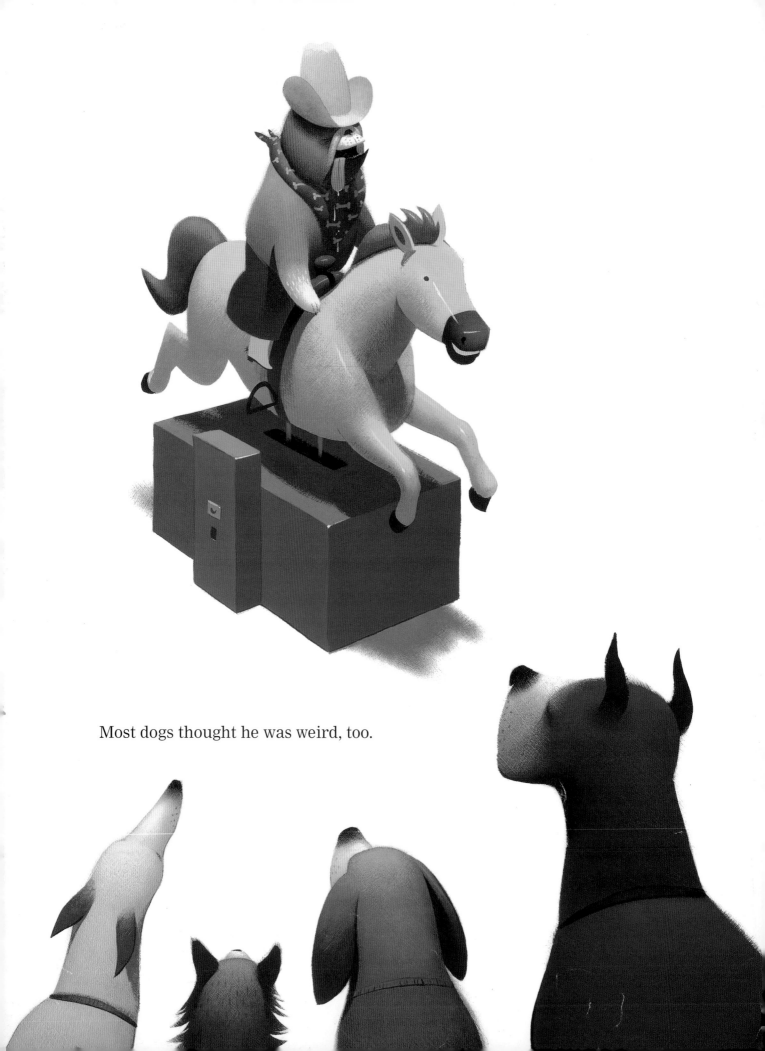

Most dogs thought he was weird, too.

Chowder wanted to be part of the neighborhood dog pack,
but the more he tried to fit in, the more he **stuck out**.

It wasn't easy being Chowder.

Chowder's only real friends were his owners, Madge and Bernie Wubbington. They didn't just *like* their bulldog, they were downright crazy about him.

"Come here, Chowder-Wowder,"

they'd say.

"It's time to put up another precious picture of you!"

The Wubbingtons had a few quirks of their own.

CHOWDER

In the beginning, Madge and Bernie treated him like a
normal dog, but Chowder had better things to do
than fetch newspapers or go for long walks.

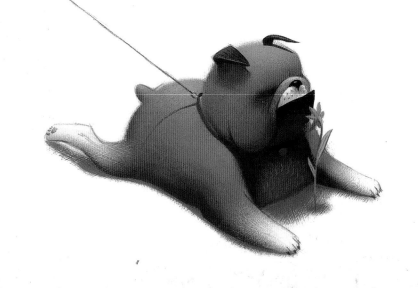

He and the Wubbingtons found their own unique ways of doing things, and no matter what they did, the bulldog always got **Strange** looks.

The only place where Chowder didn't feel like an outsider was at home, and every weekday he had the whole apartment to himself.

Madge and Bernie bought tons of dog toys to keep him company.

Chowder preferred **people** toys.

He spent sunny days on the balcony with his favorite toy of all, Bernie's **Far-Out Stellarscope**. One afternoon, while Chowder was observing another rush hour traffic jam, a brand-new billboard caught his eye.

Chowder had been to the Food Ranch a hundred times with the Wubbingtons. It was the king of all supermarkets. Inside were attractions like the Freezer Food Ravine and the Whoa Nelly Deli. And now there was a new petting zoo called the Critter Corral. Suddenly Chowder's brain was **buzzing**.

All the neighborhood dogs had said Chowder belonged in a zoo, and he wondered if they were right. He couldn't wait to meet the petting zoo animals, but a week later the Wubbingtons still hadn't gone grocery shopping.

So Chowder cooked up the perfect plan and turned his usual midnight snack into a midnight **feast!** Madge and Bernie woke up Saturday morning with empty stomachs and an empty fridge, and just like Chowder had planned, they finally took a trip to the Food Ranch.

The Wubbingtons pulled into the parking lot, and as soon as the car door opened, Chowder **scrambled** over Madge's lap and headed straight for the Critter Corral.

Critter Corral

Chowder figured this was his best chance of finding friends, and he didn't want to ruin it. He was just about to introduce himself when a red kickball rolled over to him.

All he had to do was **bump** the ball back under the fence and he knew they'd invite him to play.

But Chowder had never kicked a ball before. With the first clumsy swing of his paw, he launched the ball over the animals and into a tree! They heard it bounce around between the branches, and after one final **BOING!** it was silent. The ball was stuck.

They were still looking up at the tree when the Wubbingtons appeared.

"Get along, little doggy,"

Bernie said as he scooped up his bulldog.

"It's time to rustle up some grub!"

Before Chowder could even apologize for losing the ball, he was rolling away from the petting zoo.

Chowder was not happy.

Since he took up all of the shopping cart space, the Wubbingtons parked their pooch in the one place they knew he'd stay put. But not even dog food could keep Chowder's mind off the petting zoo.

He'd felt like a real **fool** out there, and he couldn't face the animals again unless he had their ball. But he was too short to climb the tree, and the Food Ranch didn't sell kickballs. He didn't know what to do.

Chowder was feeling sorry for himself when his belly began to gurgle and groan. His midnight feast was telling him that he needed to find a toilet, so he headed upstairs to the restroom.

While washing up, Chowder had a wild idea. He squeezed into the restroom window, and just as he'd hoped, he could see the kickball in a nearby tree.

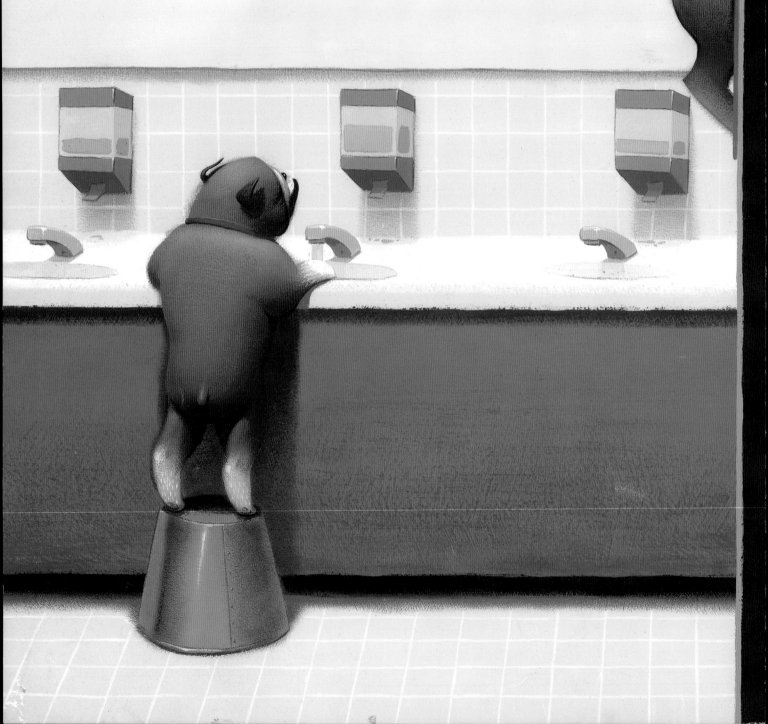

The bulldog mustered up his courage
and with one loud

**YELP!**

he popped into the air!

Chowder tumbled through the leaves and branches but fell just short of the kickball. As he dangled high above the ground, Chowder realized he had no way of getting down and no way of barking for help.

Just then he began to hear **stomping** and **snorting** directly beneath him. The sounds grew louder and closer, and suddenly Chowder felt something fluffy under his feet.

The petting zoo animals rescued him,
and they did it in *style!*

Now that Chowder had **fetched** the kickball, the animals were eager to play. Since he was the best kicker in the group, everyone wanted him on their team.

They moved the playing field farther from the trees and spent the morning teaching him all about the game.

During time-outs, Chowder showed them some of *his* favorite games.
It was a very busy morning.

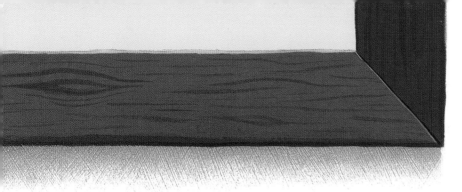

When Madge and Bernie finally tracked down their bulldog, they were happy to see that he'd found some new playmates.

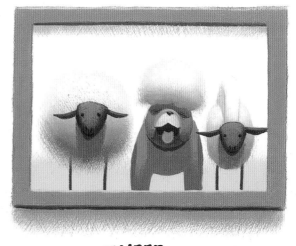

*"Say CHOWDER, everyone!"*

Madge said as she snapped a few more precious pictures for their collection.

From then on, whenever the Wubbingtons went grocery shopping, they always dropped Chowder off at the Critter Corral. And even when Chowder couldn't make it to the petting zoo, he and his friends still found ways of having **fun** together.